ALWAYS, ALWAYS

LORAH PARK MEDIA CENTER

ALWAYS, ALWAYS

Crescent Dragonwagon

Illustrated by

Arieh Zeldich

Macmillan Publishing Company
New York

Copyright © 1984 Crescent Dragonwagon
Copyright © 1984 Arieh Zeldich
All rights reserved. No part of this book may be reproduced
or transmitted in any form or by any means, electronic or
mechanical, including photocopying, recording or by any
information storage and retrieval system, without
permission in writing from the Publisher.

Macmillan Publishing Company
866 Third Avenue, New York, N.Y. 10022
Collier Macmillan Canada, Inc.
Printed in the United States of America
10 9 8 7 6 5 4 3
Library of Congress Cataloging in Publication Data
Dragonwagon, Crescent.
Always, always.
Summary: A little girl discovers that although her
parents are divorced, it in no way changes their love
for her.
[1. Parent and child—Fiction.   2. Divorce—Fiction]
I. Zeldich, Arieh, date, ill.   II. Title.
PZ7.D7824Al 1984   [E]   83-22199
ISBN 0-02-733080-X

For Jessica Casstevens, my niece,
who will always, always
be loved.

I live each fall and winter and spring
with my mother, in the city.
But every summer, at the end of school,
my mother takes me to the airport
to fly to my father,
who lives in Colorado.
It's sad in the car,
driving to the airport with my mother,
knowing I'm leaving her again.

"You'll call me when you get in?" she says.

"You *know* I will!" I say. "And you'll call me every Saturday?"

"Just like always," she says. "Cross my heart."

"I'll send you postcards of all the places Daddy and I visit," I tell her.

"And I'll send you postcards of New York," she says, "so you won't forget."

"I won't forget," I tell her, and I say, "tell Esther and Arnold and Steve good-by again for me, too." Those are all people who work in my mother's office. I see them when I visit her at work, and sometimes Esther takes me out to lunch, and once Steve signed my autograph book. On my birthday, they all sent me a card. I'll send them postcards, too, and also Nora, my best friend from school.

When my mother hugs me at the airport,
she lifts me off the ground and holds me tight,
my face against hers.
I smell her perfume
and feel her smooth clean hair
brush my cheek. Then
she puts me down and says,
"I love you. Oh, I'll miss you, honey."
"Me too," I say, "me too."

CORAH PARK MEDIA CENTER

At the door to the plane
I turn and wave one last time.
I see my pretty mother in a clean white jacket,
waving back. Her fingernails are painted red.
I remember, as I walk down the tunnel to the plane,
how she once gave me a manicure in our apartment,
and let me have my fingernails painted shiny red, too.
I thought they looked so beautiful. I told my mother,
"I can't stop looking at my hands!"
"Well," she said, "good, I'm glad you like them, though
I wouldn't tell your father. I doubt he'd approve."

My father.
I sit in the seat on the plane
and think about my father.
My father is tall
with curly brown hair
and a thick brown beard
and he smells of wood smoke
and sweat.
My father is a carpenter.
He made all the furniture
for the cabin he lives in
out in the woods in Colorado.

Last year I watched him make a cedar chest
for me to keep my clothes in when I visit.
How sweet the wood smelled when he sanded it down
to make it so smooth, there wasn't a single splinter!
He made the cabinets
in our apartment in New York, too,
before my parents got divorced,
but I was so little then, still a baby,
that I don't remember.

"The captain has turned on the no-smoking sign," says the flight attendant.
"Please make sure your seat belts are fastened."
I buckle my seat belt.
The plane is moving down the runway now, slowly,
and then faster and faster.
It goes so fast I lean forward in my seat
and then it lifts up off the ground
and I look down
and see dark water
and then streets in squares and lines
and tiny moving cars and buildings from above.
I think about my mother
driving back home to the apartment
in our small silver car.

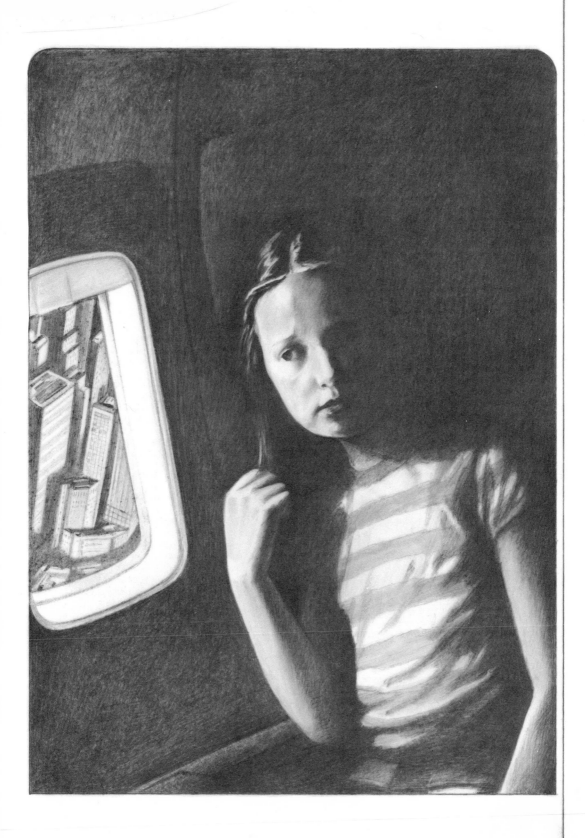

I remember how, when I call my mother from Colorado, she always says,
"It's so *quiet* with you gone! I turned up the record player
so loud the DeWitts complained,
but it still seemed too quiet."
I think about her eating dinner alone at Ming Lin's, the Chinese restaurant
around the corner, where we always eat on Thursday.
I think about how Mr. Lin will say, "Where's your little girl tonight?"
and how she'll say sadly, "She's off to visit her father for the summer,
and I already miss her."
I think about how
she'll take home the leftover Chinese food, and eat it cold for breakfast,
right out of the white paper carton.
She loves cold Chinese food for breakfast
almost as much as I love cold pizza for breakfast.

"Cold Chinese food, yuck, how can you?" I always tease her.
"Cold pizza, yuck, how can you?" she always teases back.

Now the plane
is high above the clouds.
All I see out the window
is their puffy whiteness below.
I think about my father
sweeping out the loft room, where I stay.
You climb a ladder to get there,
and the ceiling is low and slanted,
and my wooden bed has a patchwork quilt on it,
and my cedar chest is at its foot.

I think about how he'll come to get me at the airport
in his green pickup truck,
and how later in the summer
I'll ride in the back of the pickup
with Jessica, my best friend in Colorado,
to the lake.
The wind will blow through my hair.
Jessica and I will have to shout to hear each other.
Jessica's mother and stepfather will ride in front
with my father. Jessica and I
will snitch cookies out of the picnic basket,
and when Jessica's mother bangs on the glass and yells,
"Hey, you kids, keep *out* of that basket till we get there!"
we'll pretend not to hear.

I think about the plaid flannel shirts
my father usually wears,
and how when he meets me at the airport
he'll pick me up and swing me around
and how I'll smell his smell.
I remember when he taught me
how to chop wood kindling for the fireplace
with a small hand ax.
"I love doing this!" I told him. "Look at this pile I've chopped!"
"Well," he said, "good, I'm glad you like doing it. But I wouldn't tell
your mother. I doubt she'd approve."

On the way to the airport this time
I told my mother, "I'm so sad to be leaving you, but at the same time
so happy to be going to see Daddy. And at the end of the summer I know
I'm going to be sad to leave Daddy, but so happy to be coming back to you."
"A lot of life is like that," she said.
"Why did you and Daddy get divorced?" I asked her.
"Oh, you know that," she said. "We're so, so, *so* different."

They are. I thought about it.

"If you and Daddy were so different," I asked her,

"then why did you get married in the first place?"

"We didn't know ourselves too well, or each other," she said.

"It was a mistake. But *you* weren't.

You were the best thing that ever happened to us.

We have our differences, your father and I, but we both love you,

and we always will."

"Well," I said, "you may be different, but last summer he said almost the

exact same thing."

My mother laughed. She said, "Honey,
I'm sure he did,
and I'm sure he will again.
And so will I:
We both love you,
and we always, always will."

E
D

Dragonwagon, Cres-
cent

Always, always

DATE DUE

28261

	BRODART	08/90 11.95	

Lorah Park Elementary School
5160 N.W. 31st Avenue
Miami, FL 33142